This fun **Phonics** reader

belongs to

_____

Ladybird Reading

Phonics
BOOK 10

Contents

A catalogue record for this book is available from the British Library

Published by Ladybird Books Ltd
80 Strand London WC2R 0RL
A Penguin Company

2 4 6 8 10 9 7 5 3 1
© LADYBIRD BOOKS LTD MMVI
LADYBIRD and the device of a Ladybird are trademarks of Ladybird Books Ltd

ISBN-13: 978-1-84646-323-5
ISBN-10: 1-84646-323-8

Printed in Italy

The Royal Boil

by Paul Dowswell
illustrated by Chloë March

introducing the **oi** sound,
as in boy and boil

Royal Princess Joyce had a
loyal boyfriend called Floyd.

Tomorrow would be their wedding day, and Joyce was overjoyed.

Floyd was not a happy boy and
the reason was quite simple.

He had a boil upon his nose —
it was much bigger than a pimple.

Said Floyd, "The guests are sure
point, they will probably avoid me.

This boil will spoil my wedding
day. It really does annoy me."

So Floyd made an appointment
to see the royal nurse,

but her poisonous boil ointment
just made the boil worse.

Said Joyce, "Your only choice, dear Floyd, is to grit your teeth and pop it.

Or else, dear boy, the wedding's off. So do it now...

11

Not Now, Brown Cow...

by Richard Dungworth
illustrated by Andy Hammond

introducing the **ow** sound,
as in cow and loud

"Don't bother me, Brown Cow," said Farmer Brown.

When Farmer Brown came
back from town, the cows
all crowded round.

He stood there with a frown.
"Oh no, my house has burnt down
to the ground."

Megastar Mark

by Lucy Lyes
illustrated by Ken Cox

introducing the **ar** sound,
as in car

Marcus is a gardener. You may see him working in the park.

He smartens up the flower beds and sweeps up all the bark.

Yet after dark, he's Pop Star Mark, a famous superstar,

with a tartan suit, a sparkling
smile and a supercharged guitar.

Mark's army of fans scream with joy when they see their favourite star.

They charge at Mark and grab
his arm as he gets into his car.

No other artist tops the charts as often as Pop Star Mark.

So remember that when you
see him sweeping up leaves in
the park.

HOW TO USE
Phonics
BOOK 10

This book introduces your child to the common spellings of the oy, ow and ar sounds. The fun stories will help your child begin reading words including any of the common spelling patterns that represent these sounds.

- Read each story through to your child first. Familiarity helps children to identify some of the words and phrases.

- Have fun talking about the sounds and pictures together – what repeated sound can your child hear in each story?

- Help your child break new words into separate sounds (eg. sh-ou-t) and blend their sounds together to say the word.

- Point out how words with the same written ending sound the same. If d-own says 'down', what does br-own or cl-own say?

- Some common words, such as 'sure', 'love' and even 'the', can't be read by sounding out. Help your child practise recognising words like these.

Phonic fun

Playing word games with your child is a fun way to build phonic skills.

Try playing rhyming I-Spy, using oy, ow or ar words.

Ladybird Reading

Phonics

Phonics is part of the Ladybird Reading range. It can be used alongside any other reading programme, and is an ideal way to practise the reading work that your child is doing, or about to do in school.

Ladybird has been a leading publisher of reading programmes for the last fifty years. **Phonics** combines this experience with the latest research to provide a rapid route to reading success.

The fresh quirky stories in Ladybird's twelve **Phonics** storybooks are designed to help your child have fun learning the relationship between letters, or groups of letters, and the sounds they represent.

This is an important step towards independent reading – it will enable your child to tackle new words by sounding out and blending their separate parts.

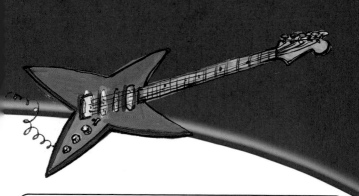

How Phonics works

- The stories and rhymes introduce the most common spellings of over 40 key sounds, known as phonemes, in a step-by-step way.

- Rhyme and alliteration (the repetition of an initial sound) help to emphasise new sounds.

- Bright amusing illustrations provide helpful picture clues and extra appeal.